PUP & PUKEY

SETH KANTNER
ILLUSTRATED BY BETH HILL

University of Alaska Press
Fairbanks

Chapter One

O ne day a baby porcupine climbed his first tree. In the green spruce branches he looked like a ball of fur with two brown eyes and twenty black claws. He was feeling a little dizzy. He held on tight and tried not to look down. The sky seemed to be swaying.

Farther up the tree, almost to the white clouds, he saw his mother. She was chewing and mumbling, "Come on, Pokey. Climb up and eat your bark."

Pokey held on for dear life. If he opened his mouth he thought his claws might open too, and he'd fall to the

ground. He rested his hairy belly across one branch and his furry face under another and peered at the treetops below. Pokey didn't want to eat his bark. He wanted to look out at the world. And he wanted to see if he could spot his friend, Pup. Pup traveled and knew things, and the breezes of fresh news that swirled in the air around him made Pokey feel bigger and more a part of the world.

Pup was a young wolf who lived in a den farther up the hill. He was sleek and silver and tall. He pranced and danced and leapt over logs. At Pup's den there was always excitement, tug-of-war and hide-and-seek games, play fighting and biting.

Pup had two sisters and two brothers, all tall and silver and brave. Their parents went on hunts and came home laden with gifts. Aunts and uncles stopped by the den to visit. Everyone stayed up late into the night, and they sang to the moon. And no one ever told them to eat their bark.

"Come up here and eat your bark," Pokey's mother said, as if she could hear his thoughts.

Without much interest, Pokey gnawed at a few branches. In front of Pup's den, he could see willows shaking and the shadows of leaping wolves. Pokey wished he knew how to prance. None of his relatives pranced or danced, and none had ever leapt over anything in their lives. Not a puddle or even a mushroom.

Pokey waved from the big tree. Just then Pup spotted him. Pup dropped the caribou tail he'd been teasing his sisters with. He licked caribou hairs off his lips and bounded down the hill, plunging through thickets.

Quickly, Pokey climbed down from the tree. He brushed spruce needles out of his hair. He stood as tall as he could on his short bowed legs. In a rustle of leaves, Pup sprang over a log, launched himself into the air, and came down with his jaws clamped on Pokey's forehead.

"Ow!" said Pokey. "Stop! Stop biting me!"

Without letting go, Pup smiled extra big to show off his new ivory. Finally, he relaxed his jaws. He grinned. "That wasn't biting. I was just resting my teeth."

Pokey rubbed at the tooth marks in his temples. He held up his other paw, covering his embarrassing yellow front teeth. "I can climb really, really high," he said from behind his paw.

Pup glanced up the big tree. Near the top he saw Pokey's mom's belly, flat and hairy. Pup grinned. Suddenly he pretended to sniff the air. He lifted his ears and whiffed his nose. "Moose!" he whispered. "Need to tell Mom!" In a rush of air and silver hair he vanished into the brush.

Wistfully, Pokey sighed and stared up the hill after him. Pokey's mom peered down.

"Eat your bark," she said softly.

Pokey wiped wolf slobber off his forehead. Slowly, he heaved himself up the tree and began to eat his bark.

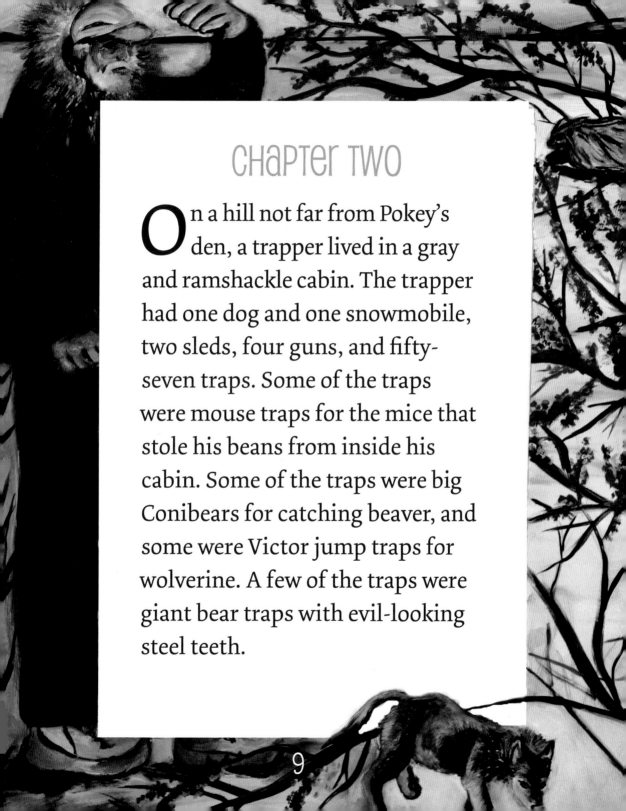

CHAPTER TWO

On a hill not far from Pokey's den, a trapper lived in a gray and ramshackle cabin. The trapper had one dog and one snowmobile, two sleds, four guns, and fifty-seven traps. Some of the traps were mouse traps for the mice that stole his beans from inside his cabin. Some of the traps were big Conibears for catching beaver, and some were Victor jump traps for wolverine. A few of the traps were giant bear traps with evil-looking steel teeth.

Occasionally the trapper grew tired of eating
fish and moose and caribou along his trapline,
and he hungered for barbequed porcupine. And
every once in a while he would get chilled on
the trapline and decide he needed a wolf skin for
mittens and a new ruff on his parka.

Because Pokey and Pup grew up in spring,
after the snow had melted, they never saw the
trapper. Although they grew up smelling the
faintest scent of smoke from his cabin and
distantly hearing the trapper's chainsaw when
the wind was right, neither Pup nor Pokey
nor their parents ever visited the other hill.
And the trapper never visited their hill.

Pup and his sisters and brothers grew rapidly.
By late summer they were tall, tough, and
unbelievably swift. Overnight it seemed,

they became huge, glorious teenage wolves. Meanwhile, Pokey only seemed to grow rounder and no farther from the ground.

Pup and Pokey occasionally still romped in the leaves and played hide-and-seek, but often now Pup brought along one or more of his siblings when he came down the hill.

"Watch this!" he'd brag to his sister or brother, and he'd launch himself into the air and come down clamping Pokey's head in his jaws.

"Ow!" Pokey whined, even though he tried not to. "Stop! Stop biting me!"

Without letting go, Pup would smile to show his siblings his startlingly white teeth. Finally, he'd open his jaws. "That wasn't biting. I was just resting my teeth. They get tired, you know."

Pokey rubbed at the tooth marks in his temples. The tooth marks were practically permanent dents now. Without thinking, Pokey held up his other paw, covering his yellow teeth. "Want to watch me climb a tree?" he said from behind his hand. But Pup was too busy. He had to hunt, or practice hunting, or howling, and soon he was bounding away and Pokey was all alone again. And he went back to eating his bark.

One evening a stranger appeared on the hill. He was a sleek, handsome porcupine with sun-bleached blond tips to his fur. He and Pokey's mom talked for a while, and then they strolled off together, and without words they made it clear that Pokey was not exactly invited.

Confused, Pokey plodded aimlessly in circles. He felt lonesome and hollow. He tried to eat his bark but had no appetite. Finally, he decided to climb up the big tree as high as he could, higher than he'd ever climbed before.

At the tippy top of the tree the wind was blowing from the south. The sky seemed to be swaying, and Pokey felt a little dizzy. He stared down the hill, wishing to spot his mom. He stared out across the tundra, hoping to see Pup hunting. Suddenly Pokey realized a sweet smell was tingling in his nose. A beautiful and alluring smell wafted on the wind. Before he could think more about what the smell might be, he heard crashing in the brush below.

Pup's furry face peered up from the ground. "Pokey! Come down! I have something to show you."

Pokey lowered himself down out of the big tree. He brushed cones and spruce needles out of his hair. He felt nervous now and ashamed in the presence of his tall, fine-looking friend. He clenched his hands in front of him and glanced over his shoulder, making sure no other wolves were sneaking up. He glanced over his other

shoulder to make sure his mom and the blond stranger were not watching from a nearby tree.

Pup picked up what he'd been hiding. "Look what we caught!" Across Pokey's toes he dropped a heavy moose leg bone and hoof.

"Ow!" said Pokey. He jumped back and swiveled, and his tail flicked involuntarily at the gnawed hoof.

Pup's grin glinted. "Don't attack with your tail! You need to learn to hunt, don't you?" He tried to bite Pokey across the forehead, but Pokey swiveled again and flicked his tail.

"Ow!" said Pup. "Ow!" He had a quill in his nose. He rolled and rubbed his face in the dirt, but the fiery quill would not pull free. "How am I going to get it out? Pull it! Pull it out! I have to go howl with my family pretty soon."

Pokey stared at the quill. He was as surprised as Pup. He plucked the quill out. "Sorry," he said. "It was an accident. Do you still want to play hide-and-seek?"

"How about chase-and-eat?" Pup growled. He snatched up the heavy hoof and trotted up the hill. Looking back over his shoulder, he mumbled, "You need to learn to hunt."

Pokey put his paws over his eyes and sat very still. His belly was hollow again with loneliness. Just then a gust of wind brought the smell swirling through the trees to his nose. Mixed in with the sweet scent was something that smelled big and watery. Pokey stood and inhaled shakily. He dusted off his shoulders and started down the hill.

At the bottom of the hill the brush thinned. The flat tundra seemed to stretch away forever. The few trees beside him were hardly taller

than he was. On the top of one of the miniature spruce a shorebird with bony yellow legs shrieked ceaselessly, as if she were pointing and telling the world Pokey was scared to leave home. Pokey *was* scared out here, but the bird only further set his mind.

He trudged south. The tundra was lumpy with tussocks and hard to walk on. In marshy areas his feet and legs grew wet. Mosquitoes bit his face and tried to bite under his armpits. His quills ached from being nervous and tense.

Under the low midnight sun, Pokey walked all evening and all night. Every time he stopped and thought of turning back, he heard Pup's words: *You need to learn to hunt.* And then he would catch another whiff of the sweet smell and walk a few more steps, and a few more.

Chapter Three

The sun was lifting into the sky when Pokey arrived at the base of a hill. Trees swayed in the wind. Watching them made him a little dizzy. He found a beaten path, and wearily he followed it. The lovely scent floated down from the top of the hill, closer and stronger now.

Suddenly the trapper's cabin stood in front of him. Along the bottom of the cabin shone a flank of the flattest, sweetest-smelling bark that Pokey had ever seen.

Cautiously, he walked up and pressed his nose to the smooth, honey-colored bark. He didn't know that the trapper called the bark *plywood* or that he was using it to block the wind from blowing under his log cabin. Pokey only knew it was the silkiest bark he'd ever touched, and the sweetest he'd ever smelled. And in his head he heard his mom advising, *Eat your bark, Pokey.*

He sank his teeth in. The taste was intoxicating. A wonderful feeling flowed in his veins. Even though he hadn't slept all night, he wasn't tired. He felt strong and tall, and very much like a hunter. He took another bite.

Suddenly a terrible roar filled the air. A dark beast lunged at him. Only Pokey's instincts saved him. He swiveled and flicked his tail. Vicious teeth raked his rump. Pokey heard a muffled yelp. He didn't stop to hear more. He

scuttled under the cabin and squeezed out of sight along the cool dirt.

It was dark under the floor of the cabin, and the beautiful smell surrounded him. From the inside, he gnawed more and more of the wonderful bark.

Pokey awoke late in the afternoon with a dry mouth, and his rump was swollen where the monster's jaws had bitten him. His feet ached, and his head throbbed. He crawled across the dirt. He peered from under the cabin. Down below the hill, shining in the sun, flowed a shimmering valley of water. Pokey was looking at his first river, and more than anything he wanted a cool drink. He began to squeeze out from under the cabin.

Suddenly a chain rattled. The dark beast snarled and lunged. Just before its teeth closed on Pokey's eyes, a collar yanked the monster off its feet.

A window opened in the cabin. The trapper leaned out and yelled, "Bonehead! Hush up!" The trapper cleared his throat, spat, and the window slammed shut.

Bonehead was brown and black and nearly as big as Pup's mom. He hung his head and glared at Pokey. He sank down in the dirt, slobbering and waiting, his eyes never leaving Pokey, blocking his only escape from under the cabin.

All evening Pokey was trapped. He gnawed at the honey-colored bark, but it was hard to swallow now. He buried his dry lips in the dirt. He piled handfuls of dirt on his pounding head.

He dreamed of water, and of his mom and Pup. When he awoke he was feverish, and he wasn't sure if the river below was real or not.

In the night Pokey crept quietly to the opening. He hoped Bonehead had fallen asleep. The first thing he saw was a fox sitting just out of reach of the dog. Pokey rubbed his eyes, wondering if it was all a dream.

The fox was pointing a black claw at one of his fine white fangs and telling the dog, "See this tooth? That's a rabid tooth. I could bite you, and you'd die."

"Not scared of a rabbit tooth," growled Bonehead.

The fox yawned. "I can't help noticing that you're growing a beard. Coming in kind of white, don't you think?"

Bonehead rubbed his face in the dirt and panted and clawed at the white quills in his lips. They only pierced in deeper. "I'm gonna be eating porcupine for breakfast," he snapped.

"Right," said the fox. "I can see that."

Pokey shivered and crawled back under the cabin.

Chapter Four

All through another day Pokey lay feverish and parched for water. The sun went down. He watched the dog eat his bowl of fish soup that the trapper had left for him.

Pokey had never seen a creature like the trapper. He had square teeth and eyes on the front of his flat face, two short legs and two long legs.

As the evening cooled, the fox returned and sat watching the dog eat.

"I've got secrets," Bonehead said over his shoulder to the fox. "I sleep

on a potato. And I'm going to be a sled dog someday."

The fox glanced at the fish soup and licked his lips. "I can see that."

Pokey closed his dry eyes and lowered his head forlornly. Just then there was a rustle in the brush. Out of the shadows Pup stepped onto the hard-packed dirt. The fox became wind—poof!—and disappeared. The dog lifted his lips in a snarl.

Pup growled softly, "Dog, move or I'll make you into a meal. Run, Pokey!" In the blink of an eye, the wolf and dog lunged at each other's throats.

Pokey was petrified. He was too feverish, too surprised, and too frightened to move. He'd never imagined such a slashing of jaws, such snarling and scrambling, such roaring and ripping. Finally, his legs tensed, and he started moving. He scurried to the edge of the hill, and down through the brush he tumbled.

Before he reached the bottom, Pup came leaping up beside him. All the pride Pokey had felt two nights ago when he left the big tree had now evaporated. "I'm so thirsty," he croaked.

Pup's ear was torn. A gash in his nose bled, and he limped, although he tried to hide it.

"Are you all right?" Pokey whispered.

Pup grinned and shrugged. "My little friend," Pup said, "didn't your mom warn you that plywood is poison for porcupine?" He turned and looked Pokey straight in the eye. "Pokey, don't eat any more of that, not ever. You have to never go back there."

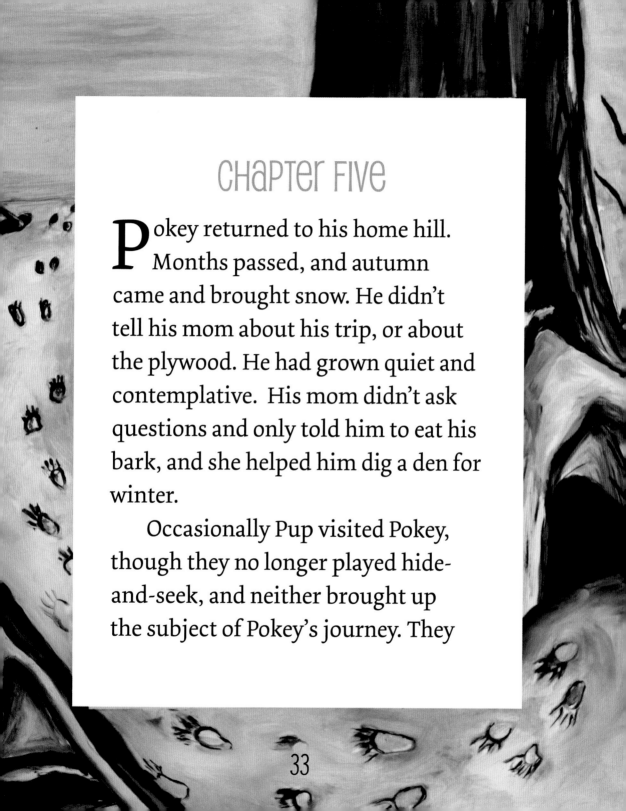

CHAPTER FIVE

Pokey returned to his home hill. Months passed, and autumn came and brought snow. He didn't tell his mom about his trip, or about the plywood. He had grown quiet and contemplative. His mom didn't ask questions and only told him to eat his bark, and she helped him dig a den for winter.

Occasionally Pup visited Pokey, though they no longer played hide-and-seek, and neither brought up the subject of Pokey's journey. They were polite to each other, and sometimes Pokey wondered if they were still friends, or something a little bit less.

One day in midwinter when the snow was deep and the air bitterly cold, Pokey heard crunching footsteps in the drift at the entrance to his den. He heard a sharp whisper.

"Hey! Anybody home in there?"

Pokey peered out into the frosty face of a stranger, a pretty young wolf.

"I'm Pup's sister," she said. "Could you please help us?"

Pokey sat up and breathed on his cold clenched claws. "What kind of help?" he asked cautiously.

"Pup's caught in a trap. None of the pack can free him. He sent for you."

"Me?" Pokey sat up straight. "Me? You sure he meant me?"

The trail was long and cold. Pokey waddled as fast as he could. Pup's sister walked in circles and waited and watched him from ahead.

"I wish caribou walked this slowly," she commented. Pokey couldn't tell if she was being nice, or spiteful, or just making conversation, but he had no spare breath to reply.

Stars were out by the time they arrived at the pack, all pacing around Pup. "Who's he?"

a wolf growled. "Pup's friend," said another. "Hurry up! Hurry!" they snapped. "The trapper's coming! Listen!"

In the distance and darkness droned a snowmobile. Pokey glanced at Pup. He could hardly believe the change in his friend. Pup crouched over a black steel object. Tears glinted in his eyes. One of his teeth had broken. When he shifted ever so slightly he whined piteously. His two toes in the trap were already frozen on the ends.

"Thanks for coming, Pokey," Pup whispered. "Sorry to wake you up. Try to hurry."

Pokey was out of breath from hurrying, something a porcupine avoids, especially in midwinter. But he noticed something else.

Unlike the rest of the pack all pacing around him, he felt marvelously calm. It was a great feeling, similar to plywood, but this feeling was better, and real. Pup must have noticed too, because he glanced at him strangely.

Pokey dug at the trap chain. He traced it to a huge spruce tree where a link was nailed.

"Stop tugging," he told Pup. "You'll need your energy." Pokey started to chew the tree trunk.

The whine of the snowmobile rose louder in the darkness. Pup's brothers howled instinctively at the sound. "Hurry! Hurry!"

The pack paced on the snow. Pokey stopped chewing. He sat up and cleaned frozen wood-chips out of his lips.

"Chew faster!" Pup's biggest brother ordered.

Pokey swiveled and looked him in the eye. Slowly he pointed in different directions. "You. You. Walk as fast as you can on three legs. Drag your fourth foot in the snow. All of you go make tracks." And Pokey turned and settled in chewing away the wood around the nails.

The roar of the snowmobile echoed in the frozen trees. The glare of its headlight flicked the black treetops. Pup whined in fear. Suddenly the snowmobile went dark. Silence filled the valley. Pup and Pokey held their breaths. From just beyond a thicket, they heard the trapper's footsteps squeak on the hard snow. Quickly, Pokey gnawed a few more mouthfuls. The trapper's steps stopped.

"Shhh," Pup whispered. His ears were up, listening.

The footsteps started again, running toward them. Pokey gnawed great mouthfuls of the frozen wood. A brilliant yellow star shone from the trapper's head, stabbing slivers of light into their eyes. Pup lunged behind the tree. The wood splintered. The nails pulled free, and he tumbled and landed with his mouth full of snow.

Pokey scurried around the other side of the tree trunk. "Run, Pup," he said calmly. "Run like you've never run before." Pokey was already climbing out of sight up under the thick branches. And on three legs Pup lurched into the darkness.

The trapper grappled to get his rifle off his back. A lightning bolt slammed into the darkness after Pup. Snow sifted down out of the higher branches. The trapper swung his headlight up the tree. His rifle lined up on Pokey's fleeing form. But then the trapper laughed, and he slowly lowered the gun.

CHAPTER SIX

In the years that followed, the trapper told and retold stories of the trapline, but his favorite story was of one cold midwinter night when he came upon a porcupine freeing a wolf from his trap. No one quite believed the trapper, but he knew the story was true, and that made it special to him.

Pokey didn't tell the story because he didn't tell stories. But he liked to climb high in the tops of trees and look at the world that he was a small part of, and sometimes he thought of the night he rescued Pup. It made him feel good.

In the mountains, Pup raised a family and taught them to stay as far away as possible from trappers. All he had to do was lift his paw with its missing toes to get his children to be quiet and sit and listen.

Only once or twice a year did Pup cross the tundra to the hill with the big old spruce. He'd peer up the tree, grin around his broken tooth, and say, "Pokey! Come down! Stop eating your bark. I have something to show you."

Text © 2014 Seth Kantner
Illustrations © 2014 Beth Hill

Published by
University of Alaska Press
P.O. Box 756240
Fairbanks, AK 99775-6240

Library of Congress Cataloging-in-Publication Data
Kantner, Seth, 1965–
Pup and Pokey / by Seth Kantner ; illustrations by Beth Hill.
     pages cm
Summary: The close friendship between Pokey, a porcupine, and Pup, a wolf, nearly ends when
they start to grow up and change according to their natures, but when Pup is caught in a trap,
he sends for Pokey to set him free.
ISBN 978-1-60223-241-9 (pbk. : alk. paper)
[1. Porcupines—Fiction. 2. Wolves—Fiction. 3. Animals—Infancy—Fiction. 4. Friendship—
Fiction.] I. Hill, Beth M., 1980– illustrator. II. Title.
PZ7.K1279Pup 2014
[Fic]—dc23
                        2013049804

Cover and interior design by Jen Gunderson
Cover illustration by Beth Hill
Photography by Joy Mitsi

This publication was printed on acid-free paper that meets the minimum requirements for
ANSI / NISO Z39.48–1992 (R2002) (Permanence of Paper for Printed Library Materials).

Printed in China

Production Date: April 24, 2014
Plant & Location: Printed by Everbest Printing (Guangzhou, China), Co. Ltd
Job / Batch #41555-0 / 702078